AT LAST

AT LAST

Ricky Allen

First Printing, 2020

Hardback ISBN-978-1-951883-03-4

Paperback ISBN-978-1-951883-04-1

eBook ISBN-978-1-951883-05-8

Library of Congress Control Number:2019954860

The Butterfly Typeface Publishing

PO BOX 56193 Little Rock Arkansas 72215

www.butterflytypeface.com

butterflytypeface.imw@gmail.com

AT LAST CONTENTS

Dedication

Foreword

Prologue 17

Chapter 1 23

Chapter 2 31

Chapter 3 39

Chapter 4 47

Chapter 5 61

Chapter 6 65

Chapter 7 71

Chapter 8 77

Chapter 9 85

Chapter 10 93

Chapter 11 97

Chapter 12 107

Chapter 13 117

Chapter 14 129

Chapter 15 133

Chapter 16 139

Chapter 17 143

Chapter 18 147

Epilogue 159

About The Author 163

Dedication

...to Enduring Hope

As It Is In Heaven

They told me how it was supposed to be.

But a living example was hard to see.

It, at times, looked good publicly.

But, what I saw and heard troubled me.

They settled for glorified mediocrity.

But, that's not how the Lord of Creation meant for it to be.

It was meant to look and function like heaven definitively.

Heaven's union is the legend for all to see.

Turn a deaf ear to them and listen to the Master of all Eternity.

Heaven intended for you to live legendary!

Foreword

As a Creative Director for a fashion brand, I am always traveling to different countries, meeting amazing people, and enjoying the diverse cultures along the journey. I had scheduled to fly out of town to Sri Lanka, famously described by Marco Polo as "one of the finest islands in the world," for scheduled business appointments. What better way to endure the 23-hour flight (including layovers) than to take a few good books with me. What happened next, some would say coincidence, and I say divine connection.

A day before my trip, I had the opportunity to meet Ricky Allen during his book signing at the Mosaic Templars Museum bookstore in Little Rock, Arkansas.

From the immediate introduction, I was impressed with his confidence, professionalism, as well as his natural articulation. He presented a summary of both of his books that was on display that afternoon - "Can These Bones Live," a practical approach to restoring love and hope within a relationship. The second book, "Beneath the Sun," takes you on a beautiful journey throughout the historic streets of Morocco and speaks directly about redemptive love between the two characters, Redo Stuart and Beatrice Napal. Halfway through his speech, I took the books off the display and said, "I will take them both. Sold." I was just sharing with a friend regarding the challenges in marriage, and I knew that both books would bring healing to his home. Perhaps I would learn some additional key points to share and encourage my friend.

Ricky's lovely wife was sitting with him during the book signing, as a powerful reinforcement of their love and commitment to each other. I was convinced and knew whatever He wrote in the books would be transparent and from the heart. I even was more than impressed.

I began reading "Can These Bones Live," on my first leg of the trip from Dallas to Hong Kong. I could not put the book down — each chapter built on the previous topic. The practical answers that addressed each situation were easy to take in and apply to my personal life. I was so impressed with the ease of the subject matter and the clarity of each resolution per chapter.

I planned to review the second book, "Beneath the Sun," once I arrived in Sri Lanka. I wanted to begin the journey poolside with the palm trees blowing and the ocean framing this picturesque setting. I wanted to create an ambiance because the book starts at a beautiful resort where the two main characters meet. This writer immediately transports you into the grand 12-day tour throughout the ancient city of Morocco. The description of the meals, and the majestic views, invoke all of your senses. The story sweeps you into the journey as you follow along with the joys and pains of the character Redo. I found myself cheering him along throughout the process. Once I completed the book, I sat spellbound – so many questions.

I had the luxury of meeting up again with the author because we live in the same city. I was so impressed with both books. I wanted to know more about the inspiration and what were some of the future goals of his project. I was blown away during our conversation. Mr. Allen's sensitivity and honesty are what he shared in preparing the books are why he can touch the hearts of the readers. I was glad to hear that the story continues, in this book, "At Last," and highly recommend reading this book.

Don't read this book only but go back and get "Beneath the Sun" so you can enjoy the entire story of Redo Stuart's and Beatrice Napal's journeys of redemptive love and enduring hope. This work will give you a different perspective on love.

I can easily see the stories of Redo and Beatrice on the big screen very soon.

Ashton Hall – Creative Director

www.asthonhallcollection.com

Little Rock, Arkansas - 2019

Prologue

Saying goodbye was hard for me to do.

"You be sweet, Redo Stuart."

"Je t'aime, Beatrice Napal."

"Je t'aime de tout mon coeur," she said while grabbing my arm, fluttering her gorgeous eyes and sharing that beautiful smile as I exited the limo.

I winked at her and blew a kiss.

My legs were heavy while I walked to my departure terminal. My feet felt like concrete blocks. My heart sunk, like a deflated balloon.

Never had I felt so vulnerable, yet so sure of something. I found that woman described in the Proverbs of Solomon. I discovered a woman whose worth exceeded rubies. I couldn't force myself to say goodbye.

Why am I leaving Morocco without her? Why didn't I stay an extra two days so we could have more time? Am I too presumptuous?

It felt like I walked miles as I arrived at the check-in counter.

"Where to?" The friendly representative asked as I fumbled through my backpack.

"Glendale, Arizona," I replied pulling out my passport.

"How was your stay?"

"One I'll never forget," I said with little enthusiasm.

The airport wasn't too crowded. Thanks to Beatrice and the limo driver dropping me off early, I felt no rush checking in and getting through TSA security.

Suddenly, I heard a voice that penetrated my ears as if someone had shoved a megaphone into them and screamed.

"Redo, wait!"

There she was, much different than anything I'd ever seen. She appeared as a blurry splotch in a dream.

Her features were unexplainable and much different from my norm.

"Don't make a promise you can't keep," she

said as time stood still.

"What are you talking about?" I responded.

"Seeing you in Paris," she said in return.

I took her in my hand as I watched others pass her by. I gently caressed her and began to cry. I felt her quiver with each gentle stroke of my hand. This impressive power was more than I could stand.

I jumped and looked around as the plane completed its rough landing and pulled me out of my deep sleep.

I could still hear the last words she spoke with teary eyes as I turned and slowly walked towards my departure terminal.

"I love you with all my heart."

What do you do when you find love that warms your heart, stirs your spirit, and shakes your soul?

What do you do when you find love that mends the depths of broken-heartedness and make you whole?

You breathe, hold on tight, and don't let go.

I departed the plane and headed to baggage claim.

As I shook my head, to clear my thoughts, I spotted my bags, passing me on the baggage claim carousel. I scurried to get them before they were out of my reach.

Suddenly, an odd feeling pressed upon me and took my breath.

RICKY ALLEN

Had I allowed Beatrice to get out of my reach?

I gathered myself, called an Uber, and headed to the place I called home.

Chapter 1

Today was a rough day.

The demands of attending meetings, seeing people, and doing things replaced the joy of being in a distant place with no one to serve but me.

It was seven o'clock in the evening.

It's quitting time, I thought.

I decided to call it a day, grab a bite to eat, and try to make it home to catch the Arizona Cardinals' season opener on Monday night football. I'm not a big sports fan; however, I enjoyed watching NFL football or, should I say, I enjoyed allowing it to watch me. I generally only make it to half time before I fall to sleep.

As I drove home, I thought *Glendale and New Hope Christian Fellowship seems different to me.*

Nothing and no one had visibly changed. Nonetheless, it seemed different.

I stopped by the mailbox and hesitated before going into what seemed to be a different home.

Once inside, I threw the mail on the kitchen table and went to get comfortable before the game. I would peruse through the mail later.

While sitting in my big chair, tossing all the junk mail, I noticed a different mail piece.

There was an envelope that had a Paris, France return address.

It was a letter from Beatrice. The excitement I felt reminded me of what it was like waking up on Christmas morning to see if Santa had left that one special toy for me.

My desire to open the letter was much like my desire then to tear open the wrapped gifts left under the Christmas tree.

Excited to read it but apprehensive to learn what it might say, I took a deep breath, grabbed my readers, opened the letter, and began reading.

My Darling Redo,

Today the sun rose, birds sprang to life, flowers emitted their fragrances, and life moved on. However, life as I had come to know it has ended.

Knowing you awakened me. This awareness came as an utterly startling revelation for me as I had no idea that I was sleepwalking through life.

I told you about my last heartbreak, but I didn't tell you that it was only the proverbial straw that broke the camel's back. My heart had been broken many times before Malcolm. And the culprit wasn't just of the romantic type. Still, I've been disappointed by love from all sources: parents, siblings, friends, and acquaintances.

Dear Heart, do you know what happens when a person stops living from an emotional standpoint? They relinquish all hope and expectation of the humankind. I believe my only source of peace was in meeting Christ. I was unaware that fear and pain had gripped me tightly and rendered me immobile. I had checked out of life.

Then, I met you.

From the start, something was startling about you. You activated something inside me. Slowly, my emotions began to breathe again. My joy began to harmonize. My curiosity sprang forth new creativity. My eyes opened, I dare to say to earthly expectations once again.

Those twelve days were as a lifetime, and yet simultaneously, it was as if we blinked, and the moments evaporated.

I looked forward to seeing you. I longed to hear your voice, and when you touched me, I felt as though I were on fire with possibility and promise.

Now that you're gone, I can't find my heart's rhythm. I see myself walking from room to room in my home as if I'm lost or searching for something. I realize that your absence leaves me feeling lost. The silence envelopes me, and I can't remember how deafening it was. Had it always been this way, and I hadn't noticed?

What do you do when you can't go back?

What happens when life as you know it has moved on without you?

How do you pretend not to know what you can never forget?

In those twelve days, I found what I'd been in search of my entire life. Somehow, before I knew you, I knew that you existed. How else do you explain missing someone you never knew? You are my soulmate. I was born to be yours. But most importantly, in the days and nights of Morocco, you became my best friend.

We talk and write ferociously, but nothing takes the place of sitting next to you, smelling you, holding your hand, and listening to your heartbeat as I lay my head on your chest.

If you can miss what you never had, you can surely agonize over what you have had. Loving you is exquisite. Missing you is almost unbearable.

I don't know what will become of me or us, but I do know that for the rest of my days, my life will never be the same. And

RICKY ALLEN

I'll always be grateful that finally, love came home.

Today the sun rose, birds sprang to life, flowers emitted their fragrances, and life moved on.

At last, I found love.

I read Beatrice's letter again and again.

Now, I know why everything seems so different.

I left a part of me the day I left Morocco.

Paris is a long way from Glendale. But neither Paris nor Glendale can keep Beatrice and me apart.

We were destined to be together.

Chapter 2

If anything has made me come close to swearing, it would be the game of golf.

"Are you ready?"

"As ready as I'm going to be," I replied as Jeff and I made our way to the first tee.

Jeff and I have been meeting more than a year each Saturday for a round of golf at Sidewinder, a renowned golf course located within Gold Canyon's Golf Resort and Spa. This fantastic place is among the top 10 wedding venues in Arizona. The beautiful backdrop of the Superstition Mountains, as well as the superbly manicured greens, add an exciting twist to a "Dream Wedding."

Why am I thinking of a wedding when I need to be thinking of keeping my tee shot in the fairway?

"Ok, let me see what you got," Jeff said while I approached my ball.

"Get your binoculars," I said before I waggled the golf club and took a swing.

I snap hooked the shot right out of bounds!

Jeff laughed. "What's gotten into you?"

"Man, I don't know. I haven't played in two weeks. I got sick in Morocco and had to cancel my planned rounds. Can I have a mulligan?"

"What?" Jeff shouted. "This is golf! There is no mercy rule."

The first nine holes were unforgiving. Jeff wasn't much better, and as we made the turn, he asked about my trip.

I didn't know where to start.

"Morocco was beautiful," I replied, taken back in time. "It was twelve days I'll never forget."

I wasn't sure how much of this experience I wanted to share. I didn't want to hear that love doesn't happen the way Beatrice and I discovered it. I didn't want to listen to words that suggest that hope is a pipe dream.

"I met an interestingly beautiful woman," I said, as I rose from my seat. "Ready to head for hole number ten?"

"You sure you want this whipping?" Jeff

RICKY ALLEN

asked as he grabbed his hat.

"I've whipped myself enough. It can't get much worse."

I laughed and walked out of the clubhouse door.

By the time we got to hole sixteen, my mind wasn't on golf. All I could think about was the letter I received from Beatrice:

How do you explain missing someone you never knew? You are my soulmate. I was born to be yours. But most importantly, in the days and nights of Morocco, you became my best friend.

I asked myself, was twelve days enough time to know, like, and trust her?

I had never been happier to finish eighteen

holes of golf as I was that day.

Jeff wouldn't let me live it down, either. But the matters of my mind were more significant than my scorecard.

For the last couple of days, I'd been thinking about my response to Beatrice's letter.

You are my soulmate.

You have become my best friend.

I was born to be yours.

Never has anyone touched my heart the way she does.

I left Morocco with hope. But now I am feeling doubt. I'd much rather preserve a friend than lose love.

RICKY ALLEN

Can this be real?

Before Morocco, I was settled on being single and had filled my life with plenty to keep me busy.

Dating wasn't a mindless activity. My family had labeled me as the "marrying kind." From my childhood through adulthood, marriage was my goal for dating.

Marred by the realities of being an adult child of an alcoholic, I struggled with trust and hope. I never saw up close and personal a man loving a woman as Christ loved His church. I never saw a man submitting to the needs of a woman as unto the Lord or a woman providing to the needs of a man as unto the Lord. I never saw a man and woman enduring the treacherous storms of life and being completely content as long as they were under the same umbrella.

Nonetheless, all I ever wanted was the kind of love that said:

When you are weak, for us, I will be strong.

When you are slipping, I will help you hold on.

When you are down, I will be there to pick you up.

When you are thirsty, drink from my cup.

When you are overwhelmed, have no fear.

You can count on me; I am always here.

Is this merely a hope against hope?

Chapter 3

After a long hot shower to wash off the sweat and the 4-hour humiliation of a bad round of golf, I decided to settle into my big chair, put on some music, and respond to Beatrice's letter.

In a world with instant communications and rapid responses, handwritten letters are pretty much a thing of the past.

Receiving Beatrice's letters took me back to a favorite past time of calligraphy. I wanted my written responses to her to be just as unique as the first moment I saw her at Rabat's Villa Mandarine Hotel.

Thanks to Arizona Art Supply, an artist wonderland located in Sun City, I have ample paper from which to choose.

I pulled out my quill, some lavender parchment paper, some gold metallic ink, and headed to the patio.

There I began to write:

Dear Beatrice,

It is always incredible hearing from you.

Encountering you has changed me and stirred my hopes for sharing my life.

I understand the idea of sleepwalking and hiding behind the pain.

It drove me to an imaginable place of perfect love and life.

Life and relationships have been nothing

like I dreamed and hoped.

I've never dated for the sport. I dated with marriage in mind, always seeking that "perfect love."

My heartbreak hasn't been from dating. My heartbreak was from a broken marriage.

I thought I had it right. We seemingly had a good life together. Little did I know, I was in a race against time and in competition with a hidden agenda.

What happens when preparation doesn't occur before opportunity?

What happens when you don't give the courtship enough time to reveal a hidden agenda?

What happens when a person spends more time trying to ensure that another person is worthy of them than they do becoming worthy of that person?

What happens when you don't acknowledge God because you don't want to accept His truth?

In many ways, I am a result of what happens.

I'd given up on the perfect love or the perfect person for me.

But the twelve days I spent with you makes me want to know you more.

Beatrice, this morning I was having coffee on the patio, watching the deer come down from the mountains to nibble on green tree foliage. I also saw a roadrunner dash across the road. It reminded me of the days we spent in Erg Chebbi.

I thought of the luxury tent city in the middle of the desert.

I thought of sand dunning and enjoying your infectious laugh.

I thought of riding camels and witnessing the spectacular sunset.

The time spent with you was a wellspring for me.

Now that I'm back in Glendale, everything seems so different.

The peace I had in being alone is now gone.

I spend endless hours wondering what

RICKY ALLEN

life could be like with a friend, partner, and soulmate all in one package.

You've shown me a preview of all that.

I felt a pleasant breeze from your sweet spirit as we basked in the Moroccan sun.

You found your way into my heart and soul.

With you, I found a place of peace and tranquility.

We were together in a place we've never been and sharing experiences we've never shared.

You touched me in ways I've never experienced before.

Together, we created moments and

memories that will never leave me.

I'm not concerned with life ever after as much as I am with life here and now.

Right now, I feel most richly blessed to have met you and even more blessed to have you as a friend and comrade.

You are right in saying, "There's no going back." I'm hopeful in moving forward and am ok with wherever we end up as long as we end up there together.

I value you and the friendship we are developing.

Thank you for being so generous in investing your time and energy into me and us.

Redo

Chapter 4

Ironically, I hadn't seen or talked to my buddy Darrell since I left for Morocco.

We met for a motorcycle ride through Southern Arizona to experience the unique charm and history of the Wild West.

We planned to take the back roads through the open desert and to visit the historic towns of Tombstone and Bisbee, the location of one of my favorite westerns, the Gun Fight at OK Corral.

I've always been intrigued by law and order.

As the story goes, settlers discovered silver near Tombstone in 1877. This place quickly grew into one of the wealthiest mining towns in Southwestern, Arizona.

Wyatt Earp, a former Kansas Police officer, worked as a bank security guard, and his brothers, Morgan and Virgil, the town marshals, represented "law and order" in Tombstone. However, they also had reputations as being power-hungry and ruthless. A close friend and temporary policeman, John Henry "Doc" Holliday, joined them. Doc Holliday was also a gambler, gunfighter, and dentist.

The Clantons and McLaurys were cowboys who lived on a ranch outside of town and were known to be cattle rustlers, thieves, and murderers.

The struggle between these two groups for control of the city resulted in a 30-second shootout that left Billy Clanton and both McLauray brothers dead.

After the 200-mile ride, Darrell and I arrived in Tombstone like cowboys needing a place to water our horses and wet our whistles.

We pulled up and parked our iron horses at the O.K. cafe. The nostalgia of this city was surreal.

We went in and claimed our seats.

The art on the walls and the waitress's attire took me back in time. I imagined being a stranger riding into town on my black stallion.

The spokes on my boots jangled as I strode in the front door of the saloon. The pearl-handled six-shooters hung on my left and right hips. The crowd shuffled and watched me as if I were there to take something that belonged to them.

"Where you from, Mister?" A scruffy fella with a tobacco-stained beard asked as I approached my seat.

"Glendale," I said, as I tipped my dusty cowboy hat.

"Folks around here don't take too kindly to strangers," he said, as he turned his head and spat on the floor.

"Sir, I ain't looking for no trouble. My horse threw a shoe, and I'm just looking for some vittles," I said as I looked around to see what I was facing.

"What are you havin' to drink, Mister?" The bartender asked as he eyed me suspiciously.

"Root beer," I said, as I flipped a silver dollar and placed it on the counter with my left hand while my right hand rested on my pearl handle six-shooter.

"So, Redo, tell me about Morocco," Darrel said, snapping me out of my imagination.

I shook my head and chuckled.

"It was more than I imagined," I replied. "I left Glendale alone looking forward to some downtime and returned alone looking forward to some changes."

"I see," Darrel said as he wiped the remnants of the Bison Burger from his mouth with his napkin. He pushed his chair back from the table and crossed his legs. By this gesture, I knew Darrell wasn't going to let me off easy.

In a way, I was glad. I've been having the day-light and darkness experience in my head ever since I bid Beatrice a hopeful, "See you in Paris."

"Man, Morocco was unforgettable. The sunsets reminded me much of the splendor of Sedona's sunsets," I said. "My first night there, I saw a woman. The sight of her seemingly caused the hotel lobby to twist and twirl as the Sedona tree trunks twist and turn due to the powerful vortex energy. I was in a place where my nature and the earth were alive with energy. The energy I felt drew her into my center focus like a cyclone. It was rejuvenating."

"What?" Darrell yelled.

"Shh, they are going to throw us out of

here," I said, trying not to laugh at his response.

Darrell responded as though he was ready to devour some dirty secret.

I knew he was someone I could confide in but wasn't sure how much I wanted to reveal about Beatrice and my time together.

Darrell listened as I shared the evening spent dancing with Beatrice and how my entire itinerary changed the twelve days I was there.

"Sounds like a great way to spend time on a trip taken alone," he replied with a little hesitation in his voice.

"Yes, but now that I'm back, it all seems like a big dream, you know?"

"When will you see her again?"

"I don't know. We've been keeping in touch thanks to modern-day technology. Beatrice is in Paris, and I'm in Glendale. It's not exactly a drive across town," I said with a touch of sharpness in my voice. "I told her that I would see her in Paris, but my schedule is crazy."

Darrell laughed and said, "Crazy should know that you are a man of your word."

We both laughed.

It was getting late in the day, so we geared up, got on our bikes, and rode on down to Bisbee. The hilly terrain surrounding the city and the art decor in the Cochise County Courthouse was spectacular. After walking around in the pedestrian-friendly town, we headed back to Glendale. I was looking forward to watching the sunset as we cruised the backroads.

Riding Sampson is genuinely the one thing that relaxes me. Every safe ride is a good ride.

Once home, I texted Darrell to see if he had made it to his home safely.

As I enjoyed the shower's piping hot water and its steam filling the room, I could hear Beatrice's voice.

"I have a way of trying to protect myself from being hurt or disappointed," she'd said.

I knew what I felt for Beatrice was real, and believe it was God sent. But I didn't know if I could trust the process.

RICKY ALLEN

I had compromised my way of protection and not being hurt by sharing my heart with her.

Now what?

Everything seems to be okay with our distant interactions.

What if we were physically in the same space for more than twelve days?

What if she was my woman and I was her man?

What if?

As I crawled into bed and began to relax, the silence started to preoccupy me.

I showed up to give and not take.

They acted as if they're entitled to the efforts I'd make.

They've seen me cry tears like rain.

They laughed and considered it fun and games.

I only wanted to provide, protect, and to cover as God appointed me.

They saw this as controlling and wanted to be free.

I was only as useful to them as my credit score and paycheck.

As their paycheck grew and score increased, they decided, what the heck.

They say I can do well all on my own.

RICKY ALLEN

God said it was not good for man to be alone.

He made us uniquely to compliment, not to compete.

Can heaven's love reflect in us for the world to see?

I tossed and turned all while these things were going through my head.

Beatrice wasn't the only one that had a way of trying to protect herself from pain or disappointment.

I've never had a problem expressing how I felt, what I believed, and what I wanted to experience in a relationship. However, this openness caused me a lot of pain.

A man once told me, if you don't share

your heart, you can't be hurt.

Ironically, I've come to realize, if you don't share your heart, you can't be loved.

Chapter 5

My order arrived today.

Many say that journaling is good for the soul.

The attention Beatrice gave to writing in that mysterious leather-bound journal left me speculating.

So, I got a journal, too.

Tonight, I write:

They say distance makes the heart grow fonder.

Who are they?

Where did they come from?

RICKY ALLEN

I can't help but wonder.

It's 107 degrees in the shade here in Glendale, but there is a chill in my atmosphere.

Is it the fear of trusting again?

Is it the fear of loving and giving my all again?

Is it the fear of loving and not being loved in returned?

What is it?

The more Beatrice and I talk, the frostier the chill gets.

Could it possibly be the reality that being with her is fondness to me?

In all that I've experienced, I haven't given up on love, but maybe it's time for me to embrace hope for the best.

I don't need a 'good' woman and no longer want to be someone's 'good' man.

I have come to understand that two 'good' people may not be the best for one another.

Everyone needs a person in their life that sees them for who they are and sees the untapped potential that brews within them. Everyone needs a person who will challenge them and celebrate them being their very best.

Beatrice awakens the man I hope to be.

Startled by my phone ringing, I closed the journal and scrambled to answer it.

RICKY ALLEN

"Redo Stuart," I said.

"Hello, Dear Heart."

I smiled like a fox eating yellow jackets after hearing the sweet, sultry response on the other end of the phone and seeing Beatrice's name on the caller ID.

Chapter 6

I was looking forward to this call and couldn't wipe the smile off my face. Thoughts of Ms. Beatrice Napal was filling my days and interrupting my nights.

"How's Paris?" I asked.

"Perhaps it's time you come and see for yourself," she responded.

I wasn't sure if she meant it or was making conversation.

Either way, I agreed with her.

"Well, I guess I'll have to do just that."

"Redo Stuart, don't get a woman's hopes up."

Beatrice and I talked about the weather, work, ministry, and current events.

However, strangely enough, she avoided further conversations about my coming to Paris like the plague.

I thought more about her suggestion as I listened to her work schedule. The agenda included an upcoming exhibition at The Centre Pompidou, Europe's most comprehensive collection of modern and contemporary art located in Paris.

The thought of being there with her was like Deja Vu. Morocco's Mohamed VI of Modern and Contemporary Art Museum was the place that I first spoke to her, and she talked to me.

Would I be distracting to her work?

Does she have time and space for me in her successful life?

"So, what are your plans once your exhibitions are over?" I asked.

"I don't have any. The planning for this exhibition has been a killer," she said. "Once it's over, I'll have a couple of weeks before my next event. I'll have nothing and no one to care for but me. Maybe, I'll get caught up on some reading or some sleep," she said, sighing.

I sensed that the rigidity of her schedule was loosening its grip.

"What about you, Redo? From the sound of it, you need a break from your busy schedule."

"You're right," I said. "Working ten to twelve

hours a day and seldom taking time off is my norm."

As I listened to Beatrice, my thoughts traveled back to a conversation my golf buddy Jeff, and I had on the golf course.

"Redo, you need to get a life and a wife."

"I have a life and am not looking for a wife," I'd assured him.

"Yes, but you need someone to share your life with," Jeff insisted.

"You know what the Bible says, Redo. He that finds a wife finds a good thing."

"You should just focus on keeping the golf ball in the fairway," I said as I laughed and nudged Jeff toward the tee box.

"The Bible also said that God put Adam into a deep sleep. When he finished making a woman suitable for Adam, he woke Adam up and presented her to him. Lord put me in a deep sleep and don't let me go sleepwalking, trying to find a wife. Wake me up when you're finished with her," I said without missing a beat.

It was clear who'd won that conversation match.

"Since I'm right, Mr. Stuart," she said, snapping me out of my thinking. "What are you going to do about it?"

Beatrice's question was direct, sassy, and penetrating.

"About what?"

"Taking some time off," Beatrice said with

feigned irritation. "Redo Stuart, are you listening to me?"

"Yes, I'm listening to you. I'm going to finish my projects, put in for a two-week leave, and come to Paris. Any more questions, Ms. Napal?" I asked, with hopes to lessen the perceived irritation.

"How soon can you get here?"

Excitement filled her voice.

Chapter 7

Hours had passed.

The more Beatrice and I talked, the more I realized that merely Facetiming and texting would no longer do.

We talked about life before our Morocco encounter, and how we had both given up hope for lasting love.

I admitted how fear and pain had dealt a blow that had knocked the wind out of me and rendered me immobile in pursuit of love and happiness.

"I understand," she said. "But, meeting you has made me come alive and hopeful. I feel that I can breathe and live again.

My curiosity has sprung forth with new creativity. My heart is open."

"Beatrice, I loved you the moment I saw you," I said. "It was the moment I saw your gentle spirit. It was the moment I saw your kind heart. It was the moment I saw your unjudgmental acceptance. It was the moment I saw your knack for laughter. It was the moment I saw your appreciation for the man I am."

"Wow," she said, fighting back the tears in her watery eyes.

"You are the one."

Beatrice's words made me wish for a private jet that would come and transport me to Paris and into her arms right away.

"Stop playing."

"I'm not playing," she abruptly replied.

"OK, to that, I say: In case you're thinking of playing me, play me. I don't mind. Play me, baby, play me, and take your time. Don't stop with just one note. Strike another two or three. Play me, baby, play me. Let's make perfect harmony."

"And when did you say you're leaving?" she said fanning and fidgeting.

"I hope to wrap things up at the office within the next two weeks."

"I'll start checking flights tomorrow," Beatrice said.

"Thanks."

"My Pleasure, Mr. Stuart," she offered with a wink and smile.

RICKY ALLEN

Beatrice and I finally said goodnight.

As I settled in for bed, I prayed and asked God for guidance.

Heavenly Father, I know there are many times when I've asked for guidance but haven't been willing to follow. But now, I'm all ears. I don't want a woman. I want to experience the woman you've prepared just for me. Order Beatrice's and my steps that we may walk the path you've predestined. Please establish our thoughts that they not be governed by lust and self-serving agendas. Help us to discover a purpose much higher than ourselves to share time and space in Jesus' name I pray.

AMEN.

Once I finished praying, I took the time to

write once again in my journal.

I know I've been called.

I am trying hard not to fall.

Watchful around the clock;

don't want to be a stumbling block.

I am your preacher man.

I need you to hold my hand.

When it's hard for me to stand,

help me to remember that I'm your Preacher Man.

You called, and I responded yes.

I'm trying hard to give you my best.

RICKY ALLEN

My brook is drying, and my soul is in drought.

Is there a raven reserved to help me out?

Your word tells me to do all with heart and with all my might.

Right now, I am weak from the fight.

I am your Preacher Man, and this, I'm sure.

Please hold my hand and help me to endure.

I closed my journal, placed it on the nightstand, turned the lamp off, rolled over, and thought of Paris as I fell asleep.

Chapter 8

Marshall and I decided to have an early breakfast. We canceled our plans for a morning run due to the torrential rain.

"When are you leaving?" Marshall asked me as we ate.

"In sixteen days," I said, taking the first bite of my pecan pancakes. I wiped my mouth as a little maple syrup escaped its crevice.

Marshall had become family to me. I've never known anyone like him. Not only does he pay attention to what I say, but he also calls me out on the things I don't say.

I met him three years ago at a men's conference for which my company handled the advertisement and communications. During the introductions, we discovered that we shared much in common.

We were both high profile professionals. We both had leadership roles in Christian ministry. We both grew up without a man to guide us in faith and family. We both were on a journey to discover love, pure and authentic. We both had an insatiable desire to become men after God's heart. We knew all too well, the fear of trust and transparency.

Because of these commonalities, we made a pact to be accountability brothers.

"You don't seem excited about your trip, Red."

The sound of my nickname felt like

someone from my childhood challenging me to confront a fear.

I grew up in a small-town village. Only my auntie and the elders call me "Red."

"I am excited, Marshall. It's just…"

"It's just what?" he interrupted. "The very mention of this woman lightens your countenance," he continued as he paused between bites.

"I'm scared."

"Scared of what?" He curiously asked.

"I'm scared of hope."

"What?"

"Marshall, when in Morocco, Beatrice and

I had many wonderful conversations. One, in particular, had to do with the games people play, and the lies society has told concerning what love is and is not. Beatrice asked me:

'So, why is a man like you single when this kind of treatment could get you any woman you want?' I assured her that I didn't engage in the social game of 'wow them until you win them.' The only treatment I was trying to give her was kindness and consideration."

"Oh, I see," he said.

"What I didn't tell her, Bro, was that I don't engage in the social game of chasing them until you catch them either. I'm not a hunter or angler that's looking for a trophy to hang on my wall. I'm not the one looking for fire-side chats about the thrills of the kill or catch. I am a man who wants to spend my time loving a woman, not chasing her."

Marshall laughed.

I continued, "There is extraordinary energy that flows between two people who interact beyond surface and games."

"From the sound of it, Red, the two of you have tapped into that energy."

"Yes," I nodded.

"So, what is there to be scared of?" Marshall asked. "Hope is not hoping if you can see it and explain it. Red, you've been praying and longing for your soulmate. Do you believe you have encountered her?"

"Yes, I do. I just don't know if I can trust what I'm feeling after only knowing this woman for seven months and sixteen days."

"Hold on," Marshall said with seriousness in his voice. "I thought we agreed to trust God in all things and not our feelings."

"You're right." I nodded.

"Have you asked God for a specific direction and confirmation?" Marshall asked.

"Yes."

"Are you waiting for direction or acting on instinct," he continued.

"I'm waiting."

"Well then, hope is nothing to fear but is

everything to embrace. Go to Paris and continue to learn of this woman you have come to know, like and trust. Get out of your way and stay in the moment," he encouraged while giving me the pact grip and walking away.

Chapter 9

I spent most of the night piddling and, pacing in preparation for my departure to Paris.

Technology had served Beatrice and me well at a distance. The hours spent Facetiming, and texting was about to culminate with an intentional visit.

I was nervous.

My flight left at 1:15 PM. The schedule has me arriving at Paris's airport (Charles de Gaulle) at 9:33 AM the following day.

I would arrive in time for Beatrice's art exhibition at The Centre Pompidou.

Beatrice had been quite kind in making

my travel arrangements. She insisted that I not stay at a hotel.

"I have a flat with two bedrooms and two baths. You are welcome to stay in the guest room, Redo, if you don't mind sharing it with my books," she'd said.

I was concerned about the appearance of this and interjected.

"That's nice of you, Beatrice, but..."

"But what?" she interrupted.

"But you don't have to do that," I said.

"Well, thank you, Sir. I am fully aware of what I have to do. Besides, if you get out of line the slightest bit, I will sick my guard dog on you."

"What? My feet are larger than Coach's tiny body. Besides, he's crazy about me."

We laughed.

Coach was Beatrice's beautiful black and tan Yorkshire Terrier. You'd think that I was calling to Facetime him whenever Beatrice and I would talk.

Beatrice and I often talked openly and extensively about boundaries. We both committed to celibacy and agreed to transparency in expressing what we felt as well as holding one another accountable for what we did.

As the Wise Man Solomon eluded in one of his proverbs, it's hard to break a three-fold cord.

We want God to be the third cord that

binds us together and agreed that we would honor Him wherever I stayed.

Before leaving Glendale, I arranged for the florist to deliver seven white roses and a box of truffles to Beatrice's office.

"What do you want on the card?" the arranger asked.

"Please add the following message," I said. "Beatrice, you've captured me like no other; You've changed my world forever. Always, Redo."

My Uber arrived as I finished the call with my florist.

"Redo?"

"Yes," I said as I verified the driver's name and vehicle license plate.

"Phoenix Sky Harbor International?" The driver looked in the rearview mirror and asked as I got in the car.

"Yes," I said, in an attempt to perk up for conversation.

"Business or pleasure?" He asked as I stared out of the window while we continued the journey on I-10 towards the airport.

"Well, I'm not sure," I said while pondering his question.

The truth was, I felt that Beatrice and I had some unfinished business. The moments spent with her were full of pleasure.

I'll have plenty of time to sort through it on the twelve-hour flight.

Beatrice also suggested I fly first-class

since the flight was so long.

"You are a big man, Redo Stuart. You don't need to be cramped on a plane for twelve hours," she'd said as we discussed my travel plans.

"OK, you win," I said as if flying first class was an inconvience.

Finally, the frequent flier miles served me well. I upgraded from coach to first-class for a nominal fee.

"This is the way to go," I said out loud even though no one was there to hear me.

It felt good having her help. Her attention to the details created wishful excitement.

As the plane taxied on the runway, I sent Beatrice a text.

Beatrice, I have boarded the plane. Thanks for suggesting first-class seating. No turning back now that I know how sweet it is! LOL. See you soon. Redo.

She replied quickly.

Yea! I'm looking forward to seeing you! I pray that you have a great flight. Beatrice.

Chapter 10

As the 747 jet soared above the clouds, my thoughts were on the twelve days spent with Beatrice in Morocco and the countless hours spent with her on the phone.

We had become best friends.

My conversations with her were effortless.

Her voice soothed me. The sight of her aroused me.

Is friendship all there is in store for us?

Would pursuing more end it all?

"Ladies and gentlemen, we are making

our final approach to Charles de Gaulle International airport. Please bring your seats forward, put away all electronic devices that exceed two pounds, and prepare for landing," a flight attendant said.

My heart leaped through my throat, not because of inflight turbulence, but because I would soon see the woman of my dreams up close again.

I took a deep breath and braced for the touch-down.

"Ladies and gentlemen, welcome to Paris, France. Please keep your seat belts fastened as the aircraft makes its way to the arriving gate, B24, gate B24. Whether you're traveling for business or pleasure, "Savourer."

The plane finally arrived at the gate and I felt glued to my seat. I waited and allowed most of the passengers to debark while I sent Beatrice a text:

Beatrice, I've made it. Debarking plane and heading to baggage claim now. Redo.

Redo, I'm happy you've arrived and will be waiting for you. Beatrice

Thoughts were racing in my head like cars racing around the Indy 500 racetrack.

Suddenly, they are interrupted as I hear my name and see her.

This time was no dream.

There she was running towards me, calling my name.

I began to run, too, while tugging my backpack and carry-on.

The excitement overtook me.

As soon as Beatrice was within my reach, I dropped my bags.

Time stood still as we held one another tightly.

Months had passed.

Although we talked when time and schedule permitted and wrote ferociously, nothing compared to this moment.

There I was holding her, smelling her, feeling her heartbeat next to mine.

It was absolutely *merveilleux*.

Chapter 11

Time stood still as we savored the moments of togetherness.

"Well, I guess we best get the rest of your luggage," Beatrice said, smiling and attempting to wipe her lipstick off my cheeks.

"Don't!" I said, and laughed.

We made our way to the baggage claim carousel. It wasn't hard to spot my belongings. It was the only piece of unattended luggage left.

"Permettez-moi de vous aider," the tall gentlemen in uniform said as he reached for my luggage and placed it on the cart along with my carry-on and backpack.

"Merci," I responded. I was happy to have my hands free to hold Beatrice's hand while we made our way out of the airport and to the car.

"I arranged for a car service," Beatrice said. She let go of my hand and interlocked her arms with mine. "I don't know that I could rightly concentrate on driving."

"Beatrice Napal, you are amazing."

"Where to Madam?" Louis, the driver, asked.

"Home," Beatrice said as if I knew where home was and as if I belonged there.

I couldn't produce much of a response; the jet-lag was affecting me.

Home, I thought. *Where is home?*

Home is where you can be safe and most vulnerable.

As Louis navigated the streets of Paris without question or GPS, it dawned on me that this wasn't just any car service.

"Here we are, Madam Napal," Louis said as he pulled under the building's portico and put the car in park.

"Merci, Louis," Beatrice said before turning to me. "Well, here we are."

The more I'm with Beatrice, the more she feels like *home.*

Beatrice's apartment near Pompidou was in the 4th district of Paris, between the bustling area of Les Halles and the historic

Marais district. I could already see there was much to enjoy outside the apartment.

The Chatelet metro station with lines 1, 4, 7, 11, and 14 goes directly to Bastille, Concorde, and the most beautiful avenue in the world, the Champs Elysees. There were several museums in the immediate area. I could see how Beatrice could settle into this place, given her love for art. This French capital is merely unique.

We exited the car, entered the revolving glass doors that led to the intriguing common sitting areas, and made our way to the elevators.

"What floor?" I asked as the doors closed.

"Fourth, please. Thank you," Beatrice said, consistently showing gratitude for my valiant attempts."

"My pleasure," I said and pushed the button.

As Beatrice placed the key in the door to her fourth-floor flat, my mind went back to Agadir as we approached the entrance to room 48 of the Sofitel Agadir Thalassa Sea & Spa resort.

I unlocked the door. Like magnets, there was a strong force pulling Beatrice and me to the center of the doorway.

"Make yourself at home," she said. The door swung open to a striking decor of quality furnishings in gray and black tones with splashes of purple. I couldn't help but smile wide at the site. Her split-level flat was lovely. The guest bedroom and bath were on opposite ends of the floor plan uniquely separated by the living and

RICKY ALLEN

dining areas.

The floor to ceiling windows created an open and airy space.

I couldn't get home out of my head. Here I am walking through a different doorway, thinking Home.

"You must be tired, Dear Heart."

"Yes, I'm a bit jet-lagged," I said.

"How about I show you to your room and run you a tub of water? Afterwards, you can lie down and get some rest."

"You don't have to do that," I said, gathering my thoughts.

"I know I don't. Just let me love you as I can, man."

"Ok, lady, woman, girl," I said.

"How do you like your water?" She asked.

"As hot as I can stand it."

While unpacking my clothes, I noticed the balcony off of my room and the courtyard down below.

"Redo! Your bath is ready," Beatrice called from the bathroom.

"You're too kind, Beatrice."

"Is there such a thing?"

I gathered my change of clothes and headed to the guest bathroom.

There were towels with my initials on them, soap and body lotion from a local

RICKY ALLEN

French boutique, a lit candle, and a note:

Redo,

Without my knowledge or consent, my heart retreated behind a mountain of pain. And while I expertly maneuvered my way through the days and nights, I admit I stopped living years ago.

You have inspired me to love and live again.

Always,

Beatrice

Beatrice's unique style, as well as attention to detail, was impressive and fit for a King.

The hot, drawn bath and sweet aroma from the candles relaxed me.

Unlike a Pharoah, I couldn't clap my hands and have attendants come to bathe me. Perhaps, this is a good thing.

Redo Stuart, you're too funny, I thought.

Chapter 12

Awakened by the smell of food, I stumbled through the unfamiliar space into the living room.

"That smells wonderful," I said.

Beatrice jumped and caught her chest.

"Oh, you scared me," Beatrice said.

"I'm sorry, BB."

"Don't be. I'm not used to anyone being here, but Coach and me."

"Speaking of Coach, where is that canine, your tenacious bodyguard?"

"Whatever," she said, rolling her eyes and

neck. "Coach is in the laundry room, down the hall to the left."

"May I go see him?"

"Sure. Dinner will be ready in thirty minutes."

As I walked down the hall, I noticed an enlarged photo of Beatrice and me with the majestic Middle Atlas Mountains as a backdrop. I recalled Beatrice's response when I asked for the selfie.

I opened the laundry room door, and Coach barked as if I were a stranger.

"What's all that noise? I thought we were buddies," I said.

Coach tilted his head and seemed to recognize my voice. He began to wag and whimper, begging to get out of the kennel.

I released the door latch and enjoyed the excitement and acceptance he was demonstrating.

It felt like home.

After playing with Coach for awhile, I could hear Beatrice calling from the kitchen.

"Redo, dinner is ready."

"Ok," I responded as I put Coach back in his kennel. "I'll wash up and be right there."

Once again, I was smitten as I went to the guest bathroom seeing the special efforts Beatrice had made to welcome me into her home. The silver towels with the black monogram uniquely complemented the black marble sink and brushed nickel faucet.

I made my way to the kitchen.

"I hope you like French Onion Soup," she said as I stood there marveling at her homemaking.

"I like it, but I love that you'd fix it for me. Everything looks and smells wonderful," I said.

"So, are you ready for your big exhibition this week?" I asked as I assisted her and then took my seat.

She smiled and sat. "I think so. Right now, I just want to think of the next couple of days with you before the event starts."

"What do you have in mind?" I asked.

"We can explore Le Marais. I want to share some interesting facts about the art, history, and architecture of the area."

"Sounds great!"

"Thanks for the beautiful flowers and delicious truffles," Beatrice said, pointing to the flowers and truffles in the center of the table.

"You're welcome."

I looked through the flickering candlelight into her beautiful eyes and blew her a kiss.

The soup and salad hit the spot. The candlelit table reminded me of the first night Beatrice and I shared dinner in Fez at the restaurant Eden at Palais Amani Hotel.

While the setting was different, the effects

were much the same, captivating.

The night view of the courtyard was intriguing. The background music created a desire in me that couldn't wait.

I pushed my chair back and walked over to Beatrice.

"Dance with me," I said as I slid her chair back and extended my hand.

"I will as long as it's slow. Can't move too fast on a full stomach."

We both laughed as she drew close to me.

Dancing was one of my favorite past times. It's not something I did publicly; however, my childhood entertainment was listening to music, playing family games, and dancing.

Beatrice was a great dancing partner.

She nestled into my arms.

We moved in harmony with the easy-listening vibes; all of my senses came alive. These were feelings I didn't realize as a young, innocent boy.

Before Morocco, it had been so long since I felt alive. I had forgotten what it was like to be warmed by the soul of a woman.

My mind went back to the garden of Eden.

What could the first man and first woman have felt when they discovered that sensual side of one another? When Adam and Eve walked and talked with God, how was there no shame in their naked existence? How could they allow the one thing that was forbidden to ruin it all?

My grandmother would often say, "Where there is smoke, there is fire."

Things were certainly heating up in me. I could also feel the heat emitting from Beatrice's body.

Ok, Redo Stuart, I said to myself, the fire will burn you if you take it in your bosom.

As Beatrice and I nestled cheek to cheek while enjoying a hot-blooded moment, I held her tight and whispered in her ear, "I want us more than I want you."

This phrase was the code for, "Let's remember and respect the boundaries that God has set so that we don't forfeit His blessings for us individually and collectively."

She sighed and said, "This is why I love you,

Redo Stuart. You take me to a place that only a woman would know. And I return from that place feeling valued more than the costliest jewel. I, too, want us more than I want you."

We winked at one another, smiled, and backed off.

It was getting late after a long day.

"I'm going to call it a night," I said after thanking her for all the outstanding efforts to make my visit special.

"OK, hold on a second," she said releasing my hand and dashing down the hall towards the guest room. I followed but waited for her to finish.

She returned and announced, "Now, your room is ready."

The beautiful rolled back bed coverings particularly moved me.

I picked up a note she had left on the pillow and immediately sensed the sweet notes of lavender.

I opened the envelope to a handwritten note that said:

Welcome Home. Rest Well.

After my shower, I climbed in bed, reread the note, smelled the envelope, and slid into the comforts of the sheets thinking:

Home should be a place of rest.

Chapter 13

I heard a slight thumping on the bedroom door.

"Coach, Coach, where are you?" Beatrice asked in a low voice.

Again, I heard the thumping on the door.

"Get away from that door," she whispered.

Suddenly, Coach barked.

Was that my clue to get up and get the day started?

"Coach, go to your kennel, now," Beatrice said.

The aroma of coffee drew me out of bed

and into the kitchen.

"Good Morning, Beatrice."

"Good Morning. I'm sorry if we disturbed your sleep," she said. "Coffee?"

"Yes, please."

"Can we go out on the balcony and enjoy coffee? It's so beautiful outside," I said as she filled my cup with the aromatic coffee.

"Sure," Beatrice said, handing me the cup and escorting toward the balcony.

The view of the courtyard from the balcony was welcoming.

The Cacti Cours Saleya, Gourdon Flowers, Rosemary Bushes, Purple Flower, Iris Flowers, and Lilies were spectacular.

"How did you sleep, Redo?"

"Without consciousness," I said.

As strange as it may sound, seldom do I sleep without consciousness. My hectic schedule creates a busy mind, even when I am asleep.

"Are you ready to get the day started?" I asked.

"Ready when you are."

"One more cup of coffee will do me good," I replied as I leaned over the balcony rails absorbing the morning sun.

Autumn in Paris was an enchanted time. The yellow, bronze, and blazing red leaves were the perfect complements to the Parisian splendor.

Beatrice, Coach, and I enjoyed the stroll in the park and along the river Seine, flowing through the heart of Paris. The autumn leaves crunched beneath our feet.

After several miles of walking, we took Coach back to the flat and decided to take a Big Bus Tour to see some major attractions.

Beatrice and I sat on the top deck. It was a bit chilly, but nothing a light jacket couldn't handle.

I was enjoying the tour, however the sight of the Cathedrale Notre-Dame de Paris was saddening.

The April fire that lasted fifteen hours resulted in devastation and temporary closure. Its historic beauty was gone;

nonetheless, restoration was in progress.

Seeing the reconstruction efforts of this monumental structure reminded me of the never-ending love that God has for His creation.

The fiery trials of life reduce many hopes and dreams to frail, charred existence in need of restoration. However, the master architect of all living things restores. The latter glory will be much more than the former.

I enjoyed the various museums and historical buildings as the Big Bus weaved through the busy streets, and the prerecorded guide offered insights.

We ended the day with a City of Lights Tour and dinner.

RICKY ALLEN

The last stop before heading back to Beatrice's home was The Galleries Lafayettes Glass Dome and the 180-degree rooftop view of Paris.

The lit Eiffel tower was breathtaking.

Beatrice and I planned to take the BATOBUS the next day and sail up and down the Seine from the Eiffel Tower to the Institute Du Monda Arabe. The BATOBUS stopped at many of the main attractions along the way.

This five-hour tour would leave just enough time to get ready for the black-tie art exhibition that Beatrice was hosting. She assured me that everything was in place. All she needed to do was show up.

Beatrice and I returned to her flat and decided to have tea before calling it a night.

Beatrice was fond of Paris' fruity black tea with vanilla, caramel, and a hint of lemony Bergamot. I settled for Japanese Sencha. Beatrice got a bottle of honey she brought from Izourki Oufella, a Morocco region that is popular for its varied and refined bee honey.

We both shipped an ample supply back to our respective homes before leaving the region.

Then we sat, enjoying the honey together as we sipped our tea.

"What is your favorite Bible story?" Beatrice asked.

"Hum," I pondered.

"I more so have a favorite scripture."

"OK, what is your favorite scripture and why?" she asked.

"Seek the Kingdom of God above all else, and live righteously, and He will give you everything you need. That's Matthew 6:33 from the New Living Translation," I said. "It is my favorite because it reminds me that God knows all of my needs and knows how to meet them. I spend my energy best seeking the One who owns everything than I do seeking things. This scripture has taught me to stay in the moment. As for my favorite story," I continued, "it would have to be the redemption story found in St. John 3:16. 'God loved the alienated world so much that He gave His only Son, that those who continue to believe in Him would not perish but have life everlasting.'"

"Thanks for sharing," Beatrice said.

"What about your favorite?" I asked.

"My favorite story is the one about Hosea and Gomer found in Old Testament book of Hosea. I like it because it's a story of redemptive love. God told this man to take on a loose woman and children and to care for them faithfully. She rejected his care, but he kept on loving and caring for them. It reminds me of how faithful God is even when we aren't faithful to Him," Beatrice said.

"Redo, do you ever talk to God about us?" she asked with gravity in her voice.

"I do."

"What do you talk to Him about?"

RICKY ALLEN

"I ask Him for wisdom, spiritual knowledge, and understanding concerning you, me, and us."

Startled by the sudden ring of my phone, Beatrice's questions were interrupted.

I recognized the number. It was T, my favorite aunt.

"It's my aunt. She'll leave a message," I said.

But she didn't. My phone rang again.

"Do you mind?" I asked.

"No, it must be critical for her to call right back."

"Hey, beautiful," I said.

T was sniffling out of control.

"T, are you ok?"

"No, Red, it's Brother."

Brother, I thought.

"Who, my dad?" I asked. "What's going on with him?"

"Baby, your dad is dead. They are going to bury him on Tuesday."

Chapter 14

I hear the voice of my auntie ringing in my ear.

"Your dad is dead."

I'm not sure what I should be feeling right now.

The man I knew little about and who was absent all of my life expired from earthly living.

"Redo. Redo. Redo!"

The projection of Beatrice's voice shook me back to the present.

"Is everything alright?" She asked with a

solemn look in her eyes.

"My dad is dead," I said, casually. "I don't know how I am right now," I said, rubbing my head.

"I'm so sorry, Dear Heart," Beatrice said and took my hand.

"He died a week ago. His wife has been trying to reach my brother and me."

Numb to the message I'd just received from 'T', I thought:

What do you feel for a man who abandoned you? I understand grown people have issues, but kids shouldn't have to suffer.

"You know Beatrice, one of the few times I saw him was at his brother's funeral. He came into the room, introducing himself, his wife, and his four-year-old daughter, my sister. He extended his hand to make himself known to me. I looked him in the eye and said, 'You don't know me, do you?' And he said, 'I can't say I do.'"

My heart sank.

Even now, as I recounted the story to Beatrice, tears fell from my eyes because of his absence in my life, not because he was dead. I didn't want to think or talk about it anymore.

"I'm going to call it a night. Thanks for a wonderful day, BB."

I kissed her on the cheek and went to my room.

Chapter 15

I finally drifted into sleep after several hours of tossing, turning, and thinking.

What was I to do?

What was I to feel?

Should I return to the States to pay my last respects to a man and a family I never knew?

Should I stay and enjoy the seven days I had reserved for Beatrice and our time together?

Later, the rain woke me up. I turned over in bed and thought, *Oh no. The downfall is going to spoil our plans to sail on the BATOBUS excursion.*

RICKY ALLEN

I could smell the sweet aroma off coffee, but the house was quiet.

As I entered the kitchen, Beatrice was sitting at the table reading.

"Good Morning," I said.

"How did you sleep?" She replied as if she heard me tossing and turning.

"Barely," I said.

I stood next to her, leaned down, and placed my forehead on top of her head.

I was hurting and not sure why. I needed Beatrice, but I wasn't sure for what.

"Would you like to talk, Dear Heart?" Beatrice was very attentive and had proven to be an excellent listener.

I felt safe to be transparent with her.

For hours, we talked about my childhood without a father. We spoke of the few times I reached out to him and how he treated me like a bother.

"You should go," she said.

"But what difference will it make? I don't know those people," I said with a trace of hostility.

"Don't do it for them. Do it for you," Beatrice said. She left her chair, leaned over the back of mine, and wrapped her arms around my chest to soothe my aching heart.

"How soon do you need to get back? I'll check the flight schedules," she said, not giving me the option to refuse.

"If I go, I need to fly out on Friday. At least I can be there for my aunt. She is the only surviving sibling. She was the only real connection I had with my dad."

As the day grew, we started making preparations for the evening event. Beatrice instructed Louis to pick us up at 6:00 PM.

Thoughts of the evening took my mind off having to cut my visit short.

I didn't want anything about me to ruin Beatrice's event. So, I told myself to stay in the moment.

Before leaving Glendale, my tailor had made sure the black Calvin Klein tuxedo fit me nicely.

I hope Beatrice likes it, I thought as I

buttoned my jacket and marveled at the perfect fit.

"Louis is here with the car," I said as the doorbell rang.

"Coming!" Beatrice shouted from her bedroom.

 Her entrance took my breath away.

The floor-length black Paris Chiffon V-neck gown was magnificent. Crystal-like stones formed butterfly wings from Beatrice's shoulders to her hips. Her earrings, clutch purse, and shoes all matched and put on a light show as she drew near me. Her perfume emitted the sweetness of glamour, beauty, and elegance.

And that she was.

RICKY ALLEN

Glamourous, beautiful, and elegant.

"Tu es beau," she said as she looked at me
and smiled.

"Tu es magnifique," I said as I winked at
her and extended my arm.

No piece of art would entreat me as much
as the sight of her at that moment.

Chapter 16

People from around the world were at The Centre Pompidou.

The Constantin Brancusi collection was her featured exhibit.

"Born in Romania in 1876, Constantin Brancusi lived and worked in Paris from 1904 until his death in 1957. Paris is where he produced most of his work. In his will, he gave his entire studio to the French state. In 1997, on the square opposite the Centre Pompidou, the French State housed his collection. The collection consisted of 137 sculptures, 87 vases, 41 drawings, two paintings, and over 1600 glass photographic plates and original prints," Beatrice so eloquently informed

RICKY ALLEN

the audience.

I marveled at how she worked the room and the pure joy that filled the air as she moved through.

Where do I fit in all of this? I thought.

Finally, Beatrice made her way back to me.

"I'm exhausted and can't wait to get out of these heels," she said, as she leaned into to me.

"Should I call for the car?" I asked as I opened my arms and gave her a big hug.

"Please do."

"You were amazing, BB."

"You're too kind," she said.

The two-hour exhibition was over, and Louis brought the car. We were on our way back to Beatrice's home.

I enjoyed the evening, but now I must deal with my premature departure. The thoughts of leaving Beatrice was more painful than before.

Morocco was a time of discovery. Paris was a time of deliberation.

What will happen now?

Will my Parisian departure return me to a wilderness of lonesomeness?

"Are you okay?" Beatrice asked, breaking the silence.

"No, I'm not," I said as I looked at her. "I hate the thought of leaving you so soon."

"I hate it too. But I understand. Your family needs you, Dear Heart."

"You have become my family. Family is not always blood ties," I said, trying to fuel the anger that would justify me not leaving.

"Dear Heart, God will not judge us by how people treat us but how we treat people."

Is this happening? I thought. *Is this woman doing what I think she's doing?*

She is speaking to my heart.

"Thanks for the reminder, BB. I needed it."

"I'm here for you," she said as she took a deep breath and nestled into my arms.

Chapter 17

The morning came.

The coffee smelled as enjoyable as it had each day I was awakened to Beatrice scrambling in the kitchen.

Coach followed his routine of coming to my door and letting his presence be known. Beatrice was the gracious host she'd been since my arrival. Louis would be here in 30 minutes to carry me to the airport.

"Will Coach and you join us?" I asked

"Have you lost you, mind, man? We would have it no other way. We're family, remember?"

RICKY ALLEN

Beatrice had arranged for me to fly to Baltimore. I would join T there, and we would fly into Topeka, Kansas, together.

I realized that Beatrice was looking out for me.

I appreciated it.

I wanted it.

I needed it.

Louis arrived and gave me one more view of the city as we headed to the airport.

"How can I thank you for the hospitality?" I asked.

"You already have, Dear Heart. Your acceptance of me is all the thanks I need," she said, fighting the tears.

"Madam, I will park the car. Text me when you are ready for pick up," Louis said.

"Thank you, Louis."

"Super de vous rencontrer, Mr. Suart," Louis said to me.

"Jusqu'a la prochaine fois, Louis," I said and shook his hand.

Not liking the thought of saying goodbye, I told Beatrice to be sweet. We were uncertain if or when we would see one another again.

Once again, I felt as though I was leaving a part of me behind.

"I will call you when I land," I said, trying to assure her that this wouldn't be the last time.

She nodded, blew me a kiss, and said, "Be sweet."

Chapter 18

I arrived in Baltimore late Saturday night and Facetimed Beatrice as soon as I got settled.

"How's the bodyguard?" I asked.

"He's missing you," she replied. "He went into the room and came out looking confused."

"Well, I grew attached to him, too."

"We miss you, Dear Heart."

"I miss you both, too."

I gave Beatrice all the logistic information for the time I will be in Topeka.

RICKY ALLEN

"How's your auntie?"

"She's coping the best she can with the help of her medication. You know, that dark liquor."

"It's good that you are there with her."

"You think," I retorted.

"Don't get smart, Redo Stuart. You're out of arm's length."

"What are you going to do?"

"I'm going to squeeze you real tight and make you beg for more," she said as she raised her brows.

We laughed.

"You promise?" I nodded and said.

"I do," she replied.

"I look forward to it," I replied in return.

We blew kisses and said, "until the next time."

Awaken to the smell of coffee and the sounds of T's voice, I got up and made my way downstairs to the kitchen.

"Good morning, baby," T said, flashing that million-dollar smile.

"Good Morning Beautiful."

"Red, I'm so sorry you had to cut your Paris trip short, but I'm happy you came."

T always showed great hospitality whenever I visit her. She says people shouldn't reserve fine dining to special occasions only. She had prepared T-bone steak, cheese grits, scrambled eggs, and French toast.

It was fine dining, for sure.

"So, how's Miss Morocco?"

She took a sip of coffee, and a bite of steak, then looked at me curiously.

"Do you mean Miss Paris?" I asked flippantly.

"No, I mean, how's Miss Beatrice Napal?"

"How did she react to your sudden departure?" T continued without giving me a chance to respond.

"She was sad but supportive."

"She insisted that I come not just for you but me as well."

"Humm, I like her," T said as she took another sip.

I sat and listened to stories and saw pictures of her and my father. However, I was numb and even sadder.

I only had faint memories and no pictures.

"I know your dad wasn't there for you, T said, interrupting my reality. But, I am proud of the man you've become. Your momma did a great job raising you. "

I didn't know my auntie growing up. However, for the past thirty years, we've had an extraordinary relationship. I could count on her brutal honesty.

RICKY ALLEN

"I didn't want to come, T. "

"I understand, baby."

"You know, his absence left me feeling unwanted, unprotected, and unsure, I continued. I've struggled to gain my identity. I wanted to hate him but couldn't."

T placed her hands on mine and said, "Red by the graces of God, you've become the unique man He purposed. I know your daddy was my brother, and I love him, but the absence of your daddy was a blessing in disguise."

T and I finished breakfast, cleaned the kitchen, and relocated to the den to watch her favorite TV show, Matlock.

I wanted to be comforting to her and my dad's family as much as I could. But I still wasn't sure what to feel.

We spent the rest of the day talking and laughing. T is sassy and humorous.

I went to bed early.

Our flight schedule had us leaving for Topeka, Kansas, at 5:30 AM Monday.

We arrived in Topeka as scheduled with plenty of time to get ready for the visitation.

Mrs. Jackie, my dad's widow, and Cathy, his daughter, and consequently, my baby sister, met us at the airport.

They recognized T. I had only seen them once in my life and felt invisible.

The family visitation was Monday evening,

RICKY ALLEN

and T was the only person I knew.

I gathered in conversation before leaving Baltimore that there was bad blood and unreconcilable differences between T and Mrs. Jackie. T was very protective of her baby brother.

"Momma, he looks just like daddy," Cathy said, pointing at me.

"That's your brother, baby," Mrs. Jackie responded.

"Oh," Cathy said.

While everyone was cordial enough, I still felt like an outsider.

It was just T and me.

Once all this is over, I would go back to

Glendale, and she would go back to Baltimore.

Then it will just be me.

Tuesday's funeral service lasted several hours.

I heard all the kind things people said about the man and dad that I never knew. The more they talked, the more I felt like a pit in my stomach was expanding to the point of bursting.

My dad was in the army and was being buried with military honors. I didn't even know that he was a Vietnam vet.

I broke out in a cold sweat.

T looked at me and asked, "Are you okay, baby?"

RICKY ALLEN

I nodded, but I really wasn't okay.

Emotions that I'd never felt were bursting to life in my chest.

The preacher concluded his sermon and beckoned for the undertakers.

I watched people come around smiling, crying, and patting the shoulder of this man I never knew. Some even bent over to kiss his cheek.

I wasn't sure what to do.

T went and viewed the remains.

The ushers had to assist her 'grief-stricken' body out of the church.

They pointed for me to come and view the remains.

I couldn't move and began to shake.

I couldn't.

I didn't want to.

Suddenly, I felt someone take my arm. The touch felt so familiar.

"It's okay Dear Heart; I'm here for you. I've got you."

I flinched with resistance and thought, *what's happening? I can't do this.*

"It's okay; I've got you."

The voice was soft and sweet, like Beatrice's voice.

But it couldn't be. I left Beatrice in Paris five days ago, unsure when I would see

RICKY ALLEN

her again.

I turned and looked. Everything was a big
blur.

"BB," I said in exhaustion.

She placed her hands on my lips and said,
"I've got you, Redo. I've got you."

She pulled me into her arms and held me
closely.

Suddenly, I knew what to do and how to
feel.

I cried without restraint for the love of
my father as I found refuge in her tight
embrace.

Epilogue

Eighteen months later.

After Beatrice's surprise appearance at my dad's homegoing service, I knew she was right for me.

After reflecting over seven months, we decided the long-distance relationship was out of season for us and that we wanted to explore a new season together.

Together, we prayed that God would reveal his perfect will for us.

The business I formed when I left Morocco was well established with a global presence.

RICKY ALLEN

I resigned as the Director of Corporate Communication and Internal Affairs at the Glendale, Arizona Hospitality Group. Pastor Rawlings and the Board of Directors of the New Hope Christian Fellowship had chosen a successor to fulfill my Associate Pastor's duties.

Beatrice took a job as an independent, International Art Curator assigned to the Paris office. In her spare time, creatives contracted her to work on their expressions of literary, visual, and performing arts.

We relocated to the same city with hopes of spending the rest of our lives together.

Austin, Texas, had fantastic museums that cater to all interests, a plethora of music venues, and an abundance of greenery, lakes, and streams.

The surrounding state parks were ideal for weekend outings with Coach.

It was a perfect place to grow a family.

We settled on a nice spread in the Texas Hill Country and made it home.

The sunsets dancing off of Canyon Lake was a constant reminder of the evenings in both Morocco and Glendale.

At last, I found love.

At last, we were husband and wife.

At last, I knew her as Adam knew Eve.

At last, she is Bone of My Bone and Flesh of My Flesh.

At last...

About The Author

Author Ricky Allen has a heart for helping others and is an ambassador for love. Anointed to lead, to teach and to motivate, this Kingdom-minded visionary eagerly gives of his time, knowledge, and heart to offer life-help and hope for all who will receive it.

Allen is not only an author but also the Founder and Sr. Pastor of the Immanuel Family Worship Center, Incorporated of Jacksonville, Arkansas as well the Owner and CEO of RELATE, LLC.

The author's passion for ministry and meaningful relationships color all aspects of his life and create in him a trailblazing spirit.

RICKY ALLEN

He is married to Annie Jean Allen. They
have five children.

Also By Ricky Allen

Live Legendary CD (Single)

Beneath The Sun

Can These Bones Live?

Can These Bones Live?

Workbook/Journal

We Specialize In building Legendary Relationships!

Butterfly Typeface Publishing

Contact us for all your publishing & writing needs!

Iris M Williams

PO Box 56193

Little Rock AR 72215

www.butterflytypeface.com

www.ingramcontent.com/pod-product-compliance
Lightning Source LLC
Chambersburg PA
CBHW071823190726
48292CB00005B/1574